THE
HIDEOUT

by Susanna Mattiangeli

illustrated by Felicita Sala

Abrams Books for Young Readers · New York

The illustrations in this book were made with watercolor and colored pencils on paper.

Library of Congress Cataloging-in-Publication Data

Names: Mattiangeli, Susanna, author. | Sala, Felicita, illustrator, translator.
Title: The hideout / by Susanna Mattiangeli; translation and illustrations by Felicita Sala.
Description: New York: Abrams Books for Young Readers, 2019. | Summary:
Hannah ignores the voice calling to her and stays in the park with the Odd
Furry Creature, making a home in a secret hideout, until, after a long
time passes, she hears the voice again.
Identifiers: LCCN 2018008414 | ISBN 9781419734168 (hardcover with jacket)
Subjects: | CYAC: Parks—Fiction. | Imagination—Fiction. | Drawing—Fiction.
Classification: LCC PZ7.M43542₃ Hid 2019 | DDC [E]—dc23

Published in 2019 by Abrams Books for Young Readers, an imprint of ABRAMS.

Printed and bound in China
10 9 8 7 6 5 4 3 2 1

Abrams Books for Young Readers are available at special discounts when purchased in quantity for premiums and promotions as well as
fundraising or educational use. Special editions can also be created to specification. For details, contact specialsales@abramsbooks.com or
the address below.

ABRAMS The Art of Books
195 Broadway, New York, NY 10007
abramsbooks.com

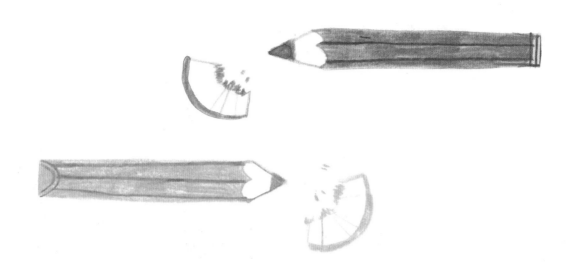

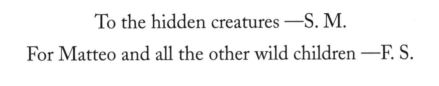

To the hidden creatures —S. M.

For Matteo and all the other wild children —F. S.

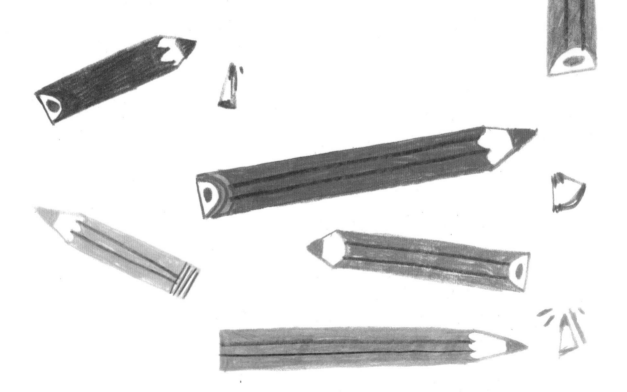

"Where are you?" a voice called.
"Hurry up, we have to go!"
But Hannah wasn't there,
and no one could find her.

Hannah heard the voice calling, but it was too late to go back.
She would live in the park, collecting lost things, drinking from the
fountain, and hunting for birds.

Maybe she'd wear a raccoon hat.

There was just too much to do; she really had to stay.

She made herself a cape out of feathers.

She made herself a bed out of leaves.

A bow and an arrow . . . What else would she need?

Some wood, a nice fire, nothing else.

The shelter was perfect, and she wasn't alone.

The Odd Furry Creature was with her, too.

She had found it behind the shrubs.
The Odd Furry Creature was always quiet
and liked to hide in the darkness.
"Are you hiding from hunters?" she asked.
But the Odd Furry Creature didn't respond.

"Are you hiding from enemies?" she tried once more.
The Odd Furry Creature was silent again.
"Can I hide with you?" Hannah pretended
to hear a yes.
She made it a cape out of feathers.
She made it a bed out of leaves,
right next to hers.

Life in the park was wild.

They ate grass and biscuits they found on the ground.

They roasted pigeons on the campfire.
They collected caterpillars, sticks, and dry leaves.

Outside the shrubs, dogs peed on trees, old ladies went for walks,
and balloons flew away.

But no one ever wandered into Hannah and the Odd Furry Creature's secret hideout. Anyone who tried would get stuck in the thick, wiry tangle of branches and leaves.

Only Hannah knew the way
through the bushes. It wasn't so hard,
if this was your home. But the more
time passed, the thicker the branches
grew, and the smaller the gaps in
the shrubs became.

In the secret hideout, there was little light. Only a few feeble noises made their way in from the outside. Whistling, bicycle bells, and voices from far away. Always far away.

Hannah and the Odd Furry Creature roasted lots of pigeons and collected lots of sticks. After that, it was perfectly quiet.

So quiet.

And only then, a voice, loud and clear,
came from who knows where.
"Where are you?" it said.

It was hard to believe, but somewhere,
someone was still looking for her.
Hannah wondered if everything was still
the same outside.
She wondered if there was anything
new to see after all this time.

Hannah grabbed the Odd Furry Creature's paw.
"Have you ever seen a balloon?"
she asked, without answer.
"Have you ever seen a dog?"
Silence again.
"Would you come outside with me and
have a look?"
Hannah pretended to hear a yes.

She took off its cape made of feathers,
folded it carefully, and put it on the bed
made of leaves, right next to hers.

They put out the fire and left their secret hideout.

They made themselves very small and crept through the
tangle of branches and leaves, careful not to get hurt.

The Odd Furry Creature came out into the bright white light.
Hannah took it for a little walk around the park.

The old ladies stared at it, and the children petted it.

The creature would get used to it, in time.

"Hurry up!" said the voice from far away. "We have to go!"

Hannah brushed away the crumbs from her eraser,
blew on the piece of paper, and got up from her chair.
"Here I am. I'm coming!" she said,
glancing at her drawing one last time.

Back in the park, the Odd Furry Creature was still sitting on a bench between dogs and balloons. The shrubs no longer seemed so thick.

From the outside, no one would have imagined that deep in the drawing,
at the end of a long road made of brown and green pencil marks,
a little girl had lived for a very long time.